Each day Rodney and friends go to the Dome-A-Roma science museum, where professor Batfish is waiting with a mission to give them.

"Today I have an assignment for the group to do, which requires your team to collect every clue."

"What's our new mission?" Rodney blurts out of turn. "Be patient, Rodney," the professor says, firm.

"A special package is coming, and I'd really like to see if you can guess what it is before the clock strikes three."

"Take out your device and follow the clues. Don't waste any time; it will be arriving real soon!"

Rochelle pulls out her tablet, and they head down the hall and then enter a dome where the trees all grow tall.

"This is the Woodland Dome, full of forests and rivers. Could this be the place where the surprise is delivered?"

"Is it a bee, a giraffe, or maybe a bear? Or perhaps it's a lion with curly long hair?"

"Yes, bees and bears do live in this dome, but giraffes and lions have a different home."

"It's good to ask questions, and this is why: we need more information to guess the surprise." Here's the first of the hints: it's black and white. Now the next time we guess, we might get it right."

So the team presses on, back on their journey, to collect the clues, but now they must hurry. They enter a tunnel with fish from the sea; there are whales and octopuses they all can see.

"Is it big or small?" Rodney
asks and ponders.

"It's small, swims, and holds its breath underwater."

"It's a fish!" Tami yells, with excitement in her eyes.

"No, but fish are sure tasty to our little surprise."

"What can it be, that's small, black and white, and finds fish delicious morning, noon, or night?"

"It can't be a polar bear," Tami says, quite amused. "He said it was small, and polar bears are huge."

"Maybe it's a seal, although they're not black and white. But they do like to swim." Boogie wonders if he's right.

As they leave the
Aqua Dome, they
feel a cold breeze.

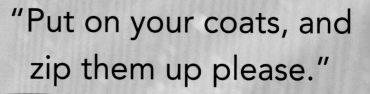

"The Arctic Dome is next;
it's cold and it's icy."

"The surprise likes it here, and it fits in nicely."

"Here's the last clue"
Rochelle says with a grin.
"It uses its wings as flippers to swim."

"It's a bird!" Rodney shouts,
"You said it has wings!"

"Yes!" Rochelle answers,
as the tablet starts to ding.

"Now let's gather the clues and put them together!"

"A bird, black and white,
that lives in cold weather!"

"It's small, with flippers,
and a really cute walk!"

"I think I've got it!" Rodney exclaims in delight. "I know of a small bird that is black and white. It swims, has flippers, and a really cute walk!"

But before Rodney can finish,
the clock chimes three o'clock.

The special delivery arrives, and what do they see? A penguin surprise, as cute as can be! Remember to ask questions and collect all the clues, and you would have guessed it's a penguin too!